Moon Mermaid and the Treasure of Friendship

By Moon Mermaid
Designed by Charles Salvador & Mike Puliz
Photography by Grant Brummet, Neil Johnson, Flashingscottsman, Miah Gonzales

www.TheMoonMermaid.com

ISBN-13: 978-0692443699
ISBN-10: 069244369X

One warm summer night long, long ago,
in the blue waters of the Mediterranean Sea,
something very magical happened. The Moon
and the Sea created... a mermaid.

Moon Mermaid

Moon was a very lonely mermaid
and spent much of her time in her sea cave
dreaming of adventures.

One day, feeling bored and blue,

she found something strange.

Strange and magical!

"*A treasure map! Just think of the adventures and all of the treasures I could find!*" she thought.

Excited, Moon left at once.

Moon swam for a long time until she finally spotted something on a rocky beach. She could not believe what she saw.

Another mermaid!

The beautiful mermaid swam over to Moon.
"Hello! My name is Mermaid Christy.
Why are you hiding?" she asked.

Moon quickly explained, "I have never seen another mermaid before. I thought I was the only one."

The two mermaids shared stories and laughed.
They taught each other new things
and became great friends.

Moon told Christy all about the map she had found, and that she was searching for treasure in these new lands. Christy replied, "I know of one of these places, and you will love it! Let's go! Follow me!"

The mermaids swam until moonrise, where they came to a mystical waterfall full of other mermaids. "These are our sea~sisters." Christy introduced Moon. All of the other mermaids were so kind and beautiful. They told Moon about the secrets of Mermaid Falls. They swam and played games.

"Do you want to know the biggest secret about Mermaid Falls?"
asked Misty and Mimi, the youngest of the mermaids.
"Yes!" squealed Moon, full of excitement. "Then come with us!
We'll show you!" The mermaids raced as fast as they
could to a nearby cove.

"This is Guinevere, one of our unicorn friends. They come to the falls to visit us. It is our job to protect them and to keep their magic safe." the mermaids explained.

Moon loved the unicorn and meeting all of her new sea~sisters. She had never been so happy.

The young mermaids told Moon
she was very close to Pirate Island
and that maybe she could find
the treasure she was searching for there.

Moon set off, swimming into the dark water,
until she saw a large shadow above her.
"What could this be?" she wondered.

Surfacing, she was amazed at what she found. It was a ship! Reaching out from above, a pirate tossed down a coin and surprised her.

"The name's Black Haven. Come on up!" The pirate invited the mermaid on to his ship, where he had been counting his coins, and showed her some of his loot.

"Pirates and mermaids aren't so different after all," Moon thought.

(we both love treasure)

The Captain enjoyed learning about the
mermaids and hearing about Moon's
quest to find treasure.

The kind pirate gave her his special locket and told her it would bring her good luck on her search. Then he insisted she go and meet the rest of his crew on the island.

Moon swam through the black
waters of Pirate Island.

She soon noticed a group of
pirates carrying huge chests
of gold and jewels onto
the beach.

The pirate crew welcomed Moon.

They sang her sea shanties, told her tales and explained that they believed mermaids brought good luck!

Moon told the pirates all about the wonderful adventure she was on, seeking treasure from the mysterious map she had found. "Aye!" the crew shouted. "We've got plenty of treasure, my dear mermaid. Perhaps one of our jewels is what you seek." The pirates offered Moon a beautiful necklace. "I love it!" she said. "Thank you! And thank you for being so kind!"

Before she left the island, one of the pirates brought her a small treasure box. "We hope you find the treasure you are looking for. If you find it, you can keep it safe in here. Good luck on your travels, lovely mermaid. You are welcome to Pirate Island any time."

Moon waved goodbye and swam away into the sea.

Continuing on with her journey, the mermaid came to a lush island covered with colorful flowers, trees, and beautiful waterfalls.

As she looked closer, she saw a happy little fairy setting up for tea.

"Well, don't just lay there hiding in the cold water. Come join me for tea," the fairy called out to Moon.

Moon wasn't sure what to do.
She never really went that far onto land.
"Well? Come on!" the fairy said.
Moon splashed up onto a toadstool and
showed the fairy her tail.

"I really can't be out of water long, or my tail will get too dry," Moon explained. The lovely fairy smiled. She leaned over the mermaid and opened a small, whimsical jar. "I give you the gift to transform."

Moon couldn't believe it.
The fairy's magic gave her legs!

"We don't see mermaids around here very often. Now you can come and visit any time you want to," said Oaklara, the gracious fairy.

As they sipped their tea, Moon thanked her new friend and promised to visit her again soon.

The mermaid loved her gifts and was having a wonderful adventure, but she couldn't figure out where this magical treasure was that she was searching for. Swimming away, Moon could see a strange glowing crystal ball in the water. "This doesn't belong here," she thought.

When she came out of the water, she was surprised to find a wizard. "Oh, you found it! You found it! How can I repay you for finding my precious crystal ball?" the wizard exclaimed.

Moon told the wise wizard of her quest. She told him of the map and all the wonderful friends she had met along the way. "I've searched everywhere, and I haven't found the treasure yet. I don't even know what I'm looking for. Now I'm tired and so far away from home." The wizard grabbed an old book and showed her. "See here? I have just the magic that can get you home."

The great wizard pointed up to the sky where a beautiful, enchanted rocking horse appeared. "This is Vlad. He will carry you safely back home."

Just as the wizard promised, the rocking horse carried Moon through the clouds, all the way back to her sea cave.

When the mermaid got home, she looked at her map and all of the wonderful gifts she had been given from her new friends. She smiled. Moon realized she had found the treasure she was seeking all along ~ the treasure of friendship.

Thank you for the many magical adventures.

Orion	Weegy Green	Chris Salemi
Josh Pettit	Captain Black Haven	Joe Droit "Marcel"
Captain Redcap	Katybear	Frank Levreau
Oaklara Nutgrabber	Ana Von Winter	Jessica Mann
Robert Hutson	Vlad	Angel
Mermaid Christy	The Dread Fleet	Capri
Mermaid Misty	Commodore Maxmillion	Kim Kaplinski
Mermaid Mimi	Jenn Czep	Shaun Muraca
Guenevere	Squee	Charyle Calvert
Mermaid Angelica Dawn	Jake Upshaw	Robert Holmes
Toni Darling	Dirk Folmer	Cat Waite
Victoria Paege	Rys Holmes	Aubrey Neiswender
Mermaid Ellusion	Briiyana Drinkwater	Emily Greene
	Kathryn Randel	

A special thank you to.

Grant Brummett	Monica Brummett & the Brummett Family	Nicole Tatlow
Mike Puliz	Alisia Mauldin & Family	Neil Johnson
Charles Salvador	Francis Lazaro	Miah Gonzales
Shannon Hernandez	Jim Boomer	Flashingscottsman

My friends and family for their love and support.

Thank you to these fin-tastic contributers.

Will Anderson	Natasha West & Family	Alsea Bluemer
Nathan Levi	Mitzi Shearer	Janet Heintz
Joshua Jones	Randy & Jeri Woodward	David Livingston
Halima Reed	Mariann Murphy	Robert Schaffner
Roland Willis	The Mauldins	Matthew Niehuis
Victoria Millee	Chris Wartenberg	Mermaid Aqua
Anna Gillings	Elizabeth Tillery	Kai Hughes
Kristopher Schindler	Brian Groven	Ross Sieber
Scott Wallack	Keelin	Blake Laivinis
Stanley Johnson	Jodi LeBlanc	Mercedes Newbanks
Lauren Saenz	Veronica Stephan	Eric Clark
Nicole & Michael Tatlow	Kelly Eckleberry	Mary Fore
Kristyn & Mikaela Schaffner	Tiana Boos	Gene Crews
	Brenna Homans	

And to you all for helping make dreams come true.

Mermaid Blessings,

Dedicated in loving memory of....

Grant Brummett

"Second star to the right
and straight on until morning,
that's where they'll find us."

Thank you for everything, you will be missed my friend.

Made in the USA
San Bernardino, CA
13 July 2017